Leonardo da Vinci

Steve Augarde
Illustrated by Leo Brown

KINGFISHER

NEW YORK

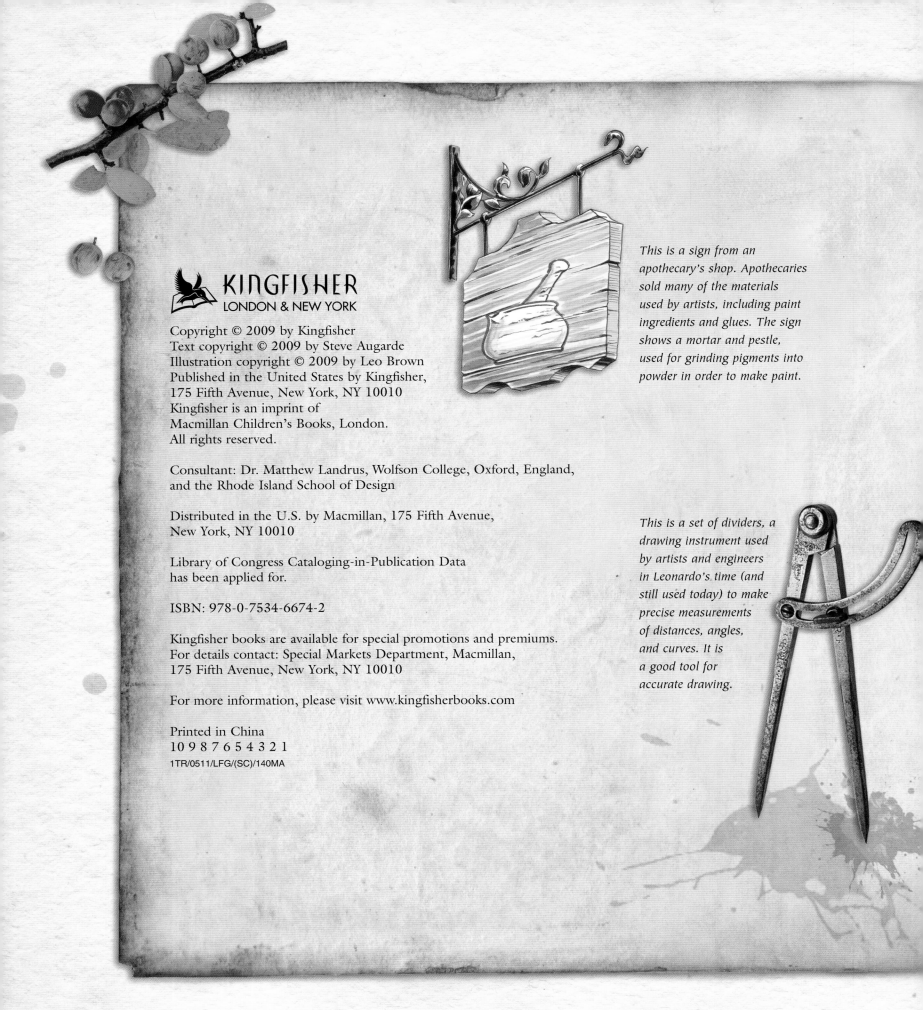

KINGFISHER
LONDON & NEW YORK

Consultant: Dr. Matthew Landrus, Wolfson College, Oxford, England,
and the Rhode Island School of Design

Distributed in the U.S. by Macmillan, 175 Fifth Avenue,
New York, NY 10010

Library of Congress Cataloging-in-Publication Data
has been applied for.

ISBN: 978-0-7534-6674-2

Kingfisher books are available for special promotions and premiums.
For details contact: Special Markets Department, Macmillan,
175 Fifth Avenue, New York, NY 10010

For more information, please visit www.kingfisherbooks.com

Printed in China
10 9 8 7 6 5 4 3 2 1
1TR/0511/LFG/(SC)/140MA

This is a sign from an apothecary's shop. Apothecaries sold many of the materials used by artists, including paint ingredients and glues. The sign shows a mortar and pestle, used for grinding pigments into powder in order to make paint.

This is a set of dividers, a drawing instrument used by artists and engineers in Leonardo's time (and still used today) to make precise measurements of distances, angles, and curves. It is a good tool for accurate drawing.

Contents

PAOLO'S DIARY

Paolo's diary entries tell of his life in Milan in 1490 and a few years later in 1498. At this time, Italy was not a single country as it is today but was made up of city-states that ruled themselves, including Venice, Florence, and Milan. These Italian cities were centers of the Renaissance, a period of great change and creativity in Europe. One of the most brilliant men of the Renaissance—an artist, engineer, inventor, scientist, and all-around genius—was Leonardo da Vinci.

June 21, 1490

I, Paolo Valenti, have now become an apprentice! Today my father has given me over and signed all the papers. I am bound for seven years to the studio of the great master Leonardo da Vinci, where I shall learn my trade. In all Milan there can be no better position. Leonardo is the painter and engineer to the court of Ludovico Sforza, and his name is known to all.

Leonardo da Vinci! How jealous my friends were to learn that I have a place in the master's studio. And as we set off from our home, in a small town near Milan, my father, too, was very pleased to stop to talk to friends and customers and to tell them where we were going. All said that I had done well for one so young and with no great education.

I am just ten years old, the middle son of a shoemaker, but I am determined to rise in this world. My father says that I should set my ambition high, and I will do my best. Perhaps I, too, will become a painter someday, as famous as my master. It is said that Leonardo had no great education either, yet look at him now. And I am able to read and write at least. Today I am beginning a journal, here in these pages. I shall record all that happens to me as an apprentice, and I shall write in it as often as I can.

This is my first day at the studio, and already I have seen much to wonder at. My father and I entered the building to find a great chamber with high ceilings and windows. There is such light that although it was early evening when we arrived, we found people still working and no candles lit. My father gave me into the care of Antonio, the chief assistant to the master. It was Antonio who showed me to my room.

Milan is one of the biggest, wealthiest cities in Europe. Thousands of skilled craftsmen and merchants work and trade there.

Everywhere there is something taking shape—so many works that I could scarce take them in as we passed through. Paintings, sculptures both large and small, pieces of theater scenery, a wonderful wooden model of part of a building, and drawings more than I could count. I have never seen such a busy place, except perhaps the market in Via Como. Can all these things be the work of one man?

Antonio

Paolo

As a busy painter, sculptor, engineer, and inventor, Leonardo has many apprentices and assistants working for him.

Carlo

As a new apprentice, I can expect to live in my master's household for seven years. I am excited to be living in such a great, important city as Milan.

I have a bed of my own. Such luxury! At home I had to share a bed with my two brothers. I have a wooden chest to keep my belongings in, and this will also serve as my writing table. Another boy, Carlo, will be sleeping in the same room. Carlo is a little older than I am—I would guess 12 or 13. He seems tired and has spoken no more than a few words. He does not want to talk about art and says only that he is hungry and waiting for his supper. I think that perhaps he cannot write.

Tomorrow I hope to meet my master and begin my first drawings—but now Carlo is looking out the window, saying that "old Dorrio" is here at last with her basket of bread, cheese, and vegetables. We must run along or we shall have no supper.

Outside the window
we hear the clatter
of carts and horses'
hooves and the sound
of people's voices.
The streets of Milan
are narrow, cramped,
noisy, and often filthy,
but I shall never tire
of being part of the
hustle and bustle
of city life.

June 24, 1490

Everyone in Milan is talking about the competition to design the dome tower for the cathedral.

Three days have gone by and I have not yet met my master. He is away on a journey somewhere—Pavia, I think—to give building advice on a cathedral. But he has also been making designs for part of the cathedral here in Milan, the dome tower, or *tiburio*. There is a competition to see whose work will be chosen. The wooden model that Leonardo has made is very beautiful, and all here are hoping that the real *tiburio* will be built to his plan. It would be wonderful if he won!

In the meantime, I have had little time for drawing. My days are filled with other work. I have to sweep the floors, clean paintbrushes, and run errands to the market. I have been allowed to help grind pigments, but not yet to mix them. Antonio says that turning pigments into paint takes many skills, and I shall be a month learning even the simplest of them.

June 27, 1490

A terrible day! I saw the great Leonardo da Vinci for the first time, but he was so angry that I scarce dared look at him. We had all been awaiting his return from Pavia and hoping for news of the *tiburio* commission. Late in the afternoon, the doors of the studio flew open and Leonardo burst in. I knew that it must be Leonardo from the way that everyone around me immediately stopped what they were doing. All noise ceased. No hammer fell, no chisel bit into stone. Only I, in my ignorance, carried on working for a few moments longer, and so my feeble grinding of mortar and pestle was the last sound to fade into silence.

Leonardo marched through the studio, his long hair flowing behind him, until he stood before the wooden model of the tower.

"Antonio! Get this thing out of my sight!" With a great blow of his fist, he struck out at the tower so that it slid from its plinth. Antonio jumped forward to save it, but he was too late and it crashed to the floor.

"Carlo, Bernardo—pick that up and set it aright," Antonio muttered, and he hurried after the master, following him into a side chamber. What could have happened?

I had a last glimpse of Leonardo as he swept his sky-colored robe around his tall figure, his angry shouts becoming muffled as Antonio closed the chamber door.

We didn't see the master again today, but at supper the whispered word went around: Leonardo da Vinci has withdrawn from the competition! We heard that Leonardo already suspected the work would not come to him. Instead the dome tower will be built by Leonardo's rival engineers, the two Giovannis—Giovanni Antonio Amadeo and Giovanni Giacomo Dolcebuono. Little wonder that our master was so angry.

I asked Carlo what all this would mean for us. Carlo was afraid, explaining that we depend upon the master for our very food. If he doesn't work, we starve. Later, Carlo shared our fears with Antonio and asked if the studio would close.

"Close?" said Antonio. "Do you think that Leonardo has no other idea in his head but this one? You are in the studio of the greatest in the land, my friend. With Leonardo, there is always another day and always another idea. No, the studio will not close!"

Brushes are handmade from wood and hair from ermines, squirrels, and pigs.

Leonardo

June 29, 1490

Leonardo is devising new methods for building canals and is making a model of a giant canal-digging crane.

Work on a clay model for a huge bronze horse monument is progressing well. I think Leonardo plans to display this model in the cathedral.

There is a different feeling in the studio now that the master is back from Pavia and working among us, and we all try harder than ever. It is wonderful to watch him at work—jumping from one task to the next with such speed that he reminds me of the street jugglers in Via Como, throwing oranges, pears, and lemons into the air and keeping all aloft somehow. One moment he is working on a clay horse—the model for a great bronze horse that will be the largest bronze statue ever cast, they say, and is to stand outside the Sforza palace. The next minute he is planning some engineering works for a new canal system, and then he leaves that to add to his ideas for defenses, curious war machines such as I never saw the likes of before. Then there are ideas for masked balls, and scenery for plays and entertainments at the palace, and tricks and amusements too many to count.

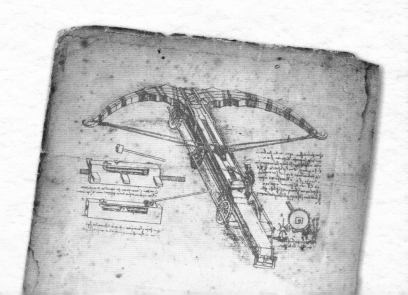

My master studies the insides of birds and beasts and insects, cutting them open in order to better understand them. He brings into the studio people he has glimpsed in the streets—those with an unusual face or some feature he wants to study. All life falls beneath his gaze, and there is nothing of this world that does not interest him. He is busy from morning till night.

When Leonardo studies dead animals, I'm glad when one of the other apprentices has to clean up the mess.

Yet sometimes he just stands and stares at a few simple lines on a piece of paper and makes just a few marks on the same small figure, or even no further mark at all. I might have swept the floor, cleaned brushes, ground pigments, and run to the marketplace for oils a dozen times, and still the sheet of paper remains almost blank. I cannot imagine what he is thinking. And this is not surprising, for when a drawing finally appears, it will be of something that none but he could have imagined. It makes my head spin just to be in the same room as Leonardo da Vinci.

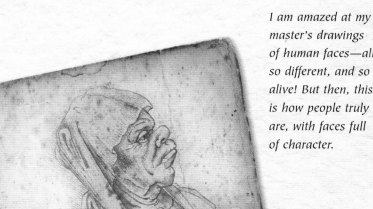

I am amazed at my master's drawings of human faces—all so different, and so alive! But then, this is how people truly are, with faces full of character.

June 30, 1490

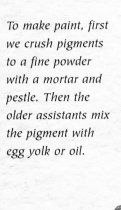

To make paint, first we crush pigments to a fine powder with a mortar and pestle. Then the older assistants mix the pigment with egg yolk or oil.

Today, for the first time, my master spoke to me!

"You, boy—you must be my newest apprentice, Paolo Valenti?" I told him I was and that I was very pleased to be here in his studio. I put down my mortar and pestle for a moment and listened to him.

My master asked whether I knew the way to the apothecary's shop in Via Tiziano, and I told him that I did. Leonardo then asked me to run an errand for him. I was to go to the shop and see if there were any green blackthorn berries to be had. I was to be sure to ask for blackthorn, not buckthorn. Leonardo was experimenting

with pigments and was searching for a special shade of green. He had already tried buckthorn, and it would not do.

Green blackthorn berries. An unusual request, but not difficult to remember. I ran all the way to Via Tiziano. I knew where the apothecary's shop was but had never been inside it. It seemed unlikely that I would find any green blackthorn berries there.

The apothecary was very old, and his shop was a curious place, full of jars and pots. Bunches of dried herbs hung from the ceiling, and the smell of these was mixed with sharper scents: perfumes and powders, acids and chemicals.

I asked the old man if he had any green blackthorn berries, and he frowned at me. He told me crossly that blackthorns, or sloes, would not ripen until the fall, and then I could buy them from the market, like anyone else. I said again that it was green unripe berries I wanted. He thought this very odd.

When I said they were for Leonardo da Vinci, the apothecary snorted. "Ah," he said. "A man who always seeks what does not exist. Tell your master that I do not keep green blackthorn berries—nor moonbeams, nor stardust, nor any such things that only he would require. I am a businessman, not a dream gatherer. Away with you."

I had to return to the studio with the bad news. Leonardo was annoyed, though not with me. He called the apothecary a fool and set me back to work.

The apothecary is an expert on herbs. He mixes remedies to cure illnesses— or poisons to cause them. He keeps many of the ingredients that artists need to make paint, and he even sells books.

July 3, 1490

Today I had my first day off, with time to spend as I liked. I had been thinking about the green blackthorn berries. Such things are not so difficult to come by. The blackthorn grows wild in the hills close to my home. Perhaps I might visit my father and mother—I could walk there in an hour or so, after all—and take a stroll into the countryside . . .

It didn't take me long to find what I was looking for. Just a short distance from home, the blackthorns were heavy with fruit, most of it still unripe. I gathered the greenest berries I could find, from the undersides of the bushes, and kept at my work until I had filled the little sack that my mother had given me.

"This is good, Paolo," she said. "I don't understand what anyone would want with such things, but you have tried to help— and a helpful boy will always be looked upon kindly."

This evening, when I returned to the studio, I gave my green berries to Leonardo. He was very surprised and pleased that I had gathered these for him on my day off. He said they were exactly as he would wish, and he took a handful of the berries and studied them. I asked him how this unripe fruit would be used.

"Some I shall dry and then mix into pigments. Some I shall boil and see what dye might be made from them. I heard of this when I was in Pavia, that from the blackthorn a type of green pigment might be extracted. Now we shall see what colors I can make with these. Are you interested in such things?"

I said that I tried to be interested in all things, and my master seemed pleased at this. He told me that a curious mind is at the root of all that an artist is and does.

"Put away your broom for a while," he said, "and bring me some of your drawings. Let us see how you use your time here."

Of course I was very happy—but also very nervous. What if my master should think my time at the studio wasted? Leonardo studied my drawings one by one. He remained silent until he came to the end.

"But these are good, Paolo," he said. "They're very good indeed. I can see that you deserve your place here, and perhaps a little more attention from now on."

Then my master promised that the next time he visited the palace I should accompany him as his assistant. I might find it interesting, he said, and it would be a little reward for bringing him the berries.

Praise from Leonardo, and a trip to the palace! How my fortunes have improved.

Salaì

July 24, 1490

Carlo and I have had our peace disrupted. A new apprentice arrived two days ago and is to share our chamber for the time being. His name is Gian Giacomo Caprotti di Oreno, if you please, and I never saw such a vain little curly-haired creature before in my life.

Giacomo is only ten years old, like me—and nothing but a scruffy street urchin—yet he struts and preens himself like a young peacock, walking around the place as though he owns it. What can Leonardo be thinking of taking on such a student? People say he is beautiful and might be useful as a model for cherubim and such. I can't think that he will serve any other purpose.

He has been with us for only two days, and already he is in disgrace. Leonardo had put aside some money in order to buy this new boy some decent clothes, and now the boy has stolen the money: four silver *soldi*! But instead of getting rid of this thieving scalawag, Leonardo calls him *Il Salaino*, or *Salaì*—the Little Devil—and allows him to stay! I don't understand it. If Carlo or I had ever dared behave in this way, we would have been out on our ears.

Salaì—he is well named. We shall all have to look after our valuables from now on. I have taken to hiding this journal beneath a loose floorboard each night for fear that it might be spoiled or go missing.

July 29, 1490

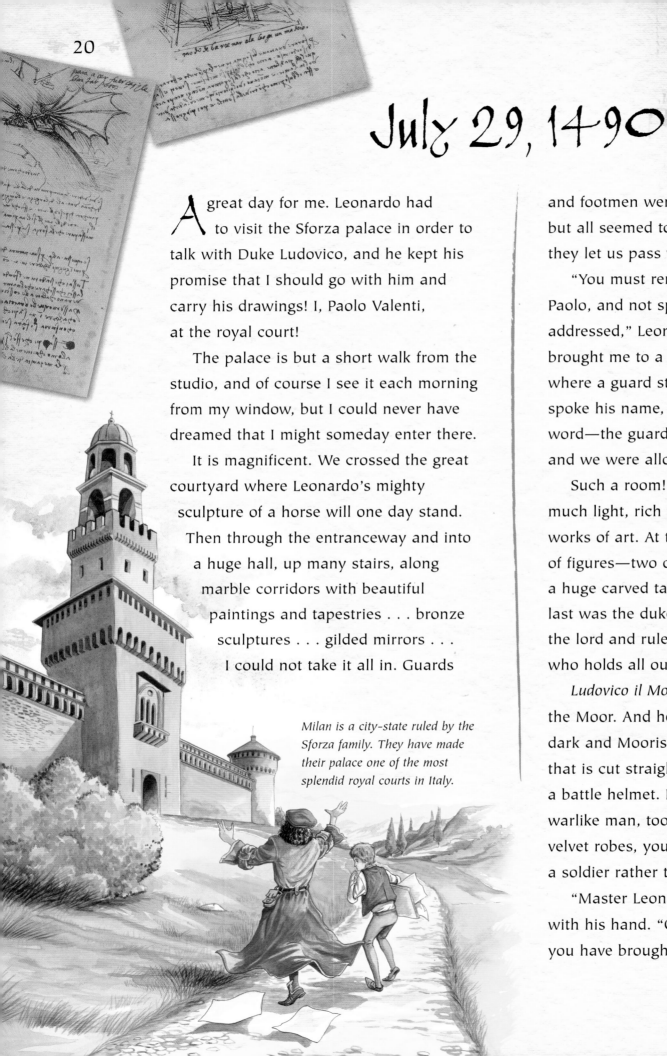

A great day for me. Leonardo had to visit the Sforza palace in order to talk with Duke Ludovico, and he kept his promise that I should go with him and carry his drawings! I, Paolo Valenti, at the royal court!

The palace is but a short walk from the studio, and of course I see it each morning from my window, but I could never have dreamed that I might someday enter there.

It is magnificent. We crossed the great courtyard where Leonardo's mighty sculpture of a horse will one day stand. Then through the entranceway and into a huge hall, up many stairs, along marble corridors with beautiful paintings and tapestries . . . bronze sculptures . . . gilded mirrors . . . I could not take it all in. Guards

Milan is a city-state ruled by the Sforza family. They have made their palace one of the most splendid royal courts in Italy.

and footmen were positioned at every turn, but all seemed to recognize Leonardo, and they let us pass without a word.

"You must remain in the background, Paolo, and not speak unless you are addressed," Leonardo warned. My master brought me to a pair of high gilded doors where a guard stood on either side. He spoke his name, and it was like a magic word—the guards opened a door apiece, and we were allowed to enter.

Such a room! Tall windows that let in much light, rich furnishings, and yet more works of art. At the far end was a group of figures—two or three standing beside a huge carved table and one seated. This last was the duke of Bari, Ludovico Sforza, the lord and ruler of Milan and the man who holds all our fates in his hands.

Ludovico il Moro they call him: Ludovico the Moor. And he is well named, being very dark and Moorish looking, with black hair that is cut straight across his forehead like a battle helmet. He looks like a powerful, warlike man, too—if it weren't for his velvet robes, you might mistake him for a soldier rather than a duke.

"Master Leonardo." The Duke beckoned with his hand. "Come. Show me what you have brought."

Duke Ludovico

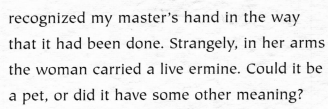

We arrived early on the summer evening, and the duke and his courtiers were just beginning their supper. There was much rich food, wine, and glistening ripe cherries.

Leonardo took some of his rolled-up drawings from me and stepped forward. I stayed to the background, of course, and waited. Leonardo spread his drawings before the duke, and all leaned over them to look. The duke and his courtiers murmured in low voices, and I could hear only part of what was being said.

"And this? A device for digging canals? Hmm. Such things are all very well while there is peace, Leonardo, but I must also think of our defenses. War is always a possibility, and I need new ideas . . ."

Nobody took any notice of me. I looked around the room and saw a portrait upon an easel. It was of a woman, and the painting was beautiful. I thought I

recognized my master's hand in the way that it had been done. Strangely, in her arms the woman carried a live ermine. Could it be a pet, or did it have some other meaning?

". . . and I'll not be outdone by those Medicis of Florence. It shall be Milan, not Florence, that is looked upon as the jewel among the Italian cities. We must have the best, Master Leonardo, the best! What of the costumes for our tournament? What can you show me?"

On and on they talked. Sometimes the duke's voice rose in delight; sometimes he shouted in anger.

"Why is this horse taking so long? Do I not pay you?"

I could see that Ludovico Sforza might not be an easy man to deal with. I saw also how our fortunes depended upon pleasing him and how difficult it was to be an artist and engineer at a royal court— even for someone as great as my master.

On the way home, I asked Leonardo about the woman with the ermine. Was it a painting of Princess Beatrice, I wondered, the woman whom the duke was going to marry?

"No, Paolo. That is my portrait of Cecilia Gallerani, the woman whom the duke would *like* to marry."

It seemed to me that life could be very complicated—for people like my master, but for dukes, too.

Cecilia Gallerani, the woman in the painting, is an important person at court. My master says she is very charming and intelligent and talked to him about art and music when she sat for her portrait.

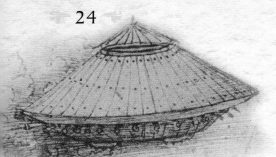

August 4, 1490

I was right to be suspicious of Salaì. Some shoes belonging to Antonio have gone missing. Salaì denies everything. He stands before Antonio with big tears in his eyes and says that he has learned his lesson and that he would never ever do such a thing. I don't believe a word of it, and neither does Carlo. Neither of us can prove anything, but as soon as Antonio's back is turned, Salaì is his usual smirking self.

Even worse, he has gotten Carlo and me in trouble with Antonio. This afternoon Salaì came to me with a message from Antonio, saying that I was to find Carlo and send him to the market to buy a dozen goldfish—*pesci rossi.*

A dozen goldfish? I thought this very odd and asked Salaì whether he was really sure. He insisted he was—and that I was to tell Carlo to be quick about it. Nothing that our master requires would surprise us, so I gave Carlo the message, and he eventually returned with the fish—and much time and trouble it took him to get them.

Now Antonio is angry. It turns out he sent for a dozen ripe peaches—*pesche rosse*—and he's furious that all these hours later Carlo brought him goldfish! Was it some kind of joke?

Poor Carlo. Everyone is laughing at him for being such a fool, and I have to take the blame for misleading him.

Of course Salaì swears he gave the correct message to me.

Carlo and I fetch eggs, berries, oils, precious pigment—even squirrel skins—for our master. But goldfish? This was something new.

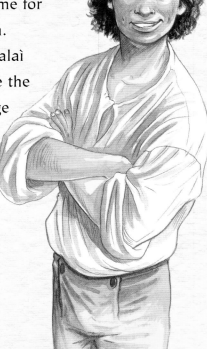

August 6, 1490

There are many other artists in Milan besides Leonardo da Vinci, and all would like to take over his position if they could. Leonardo therefore has to please his royal patron, Duke Ludovico Sforza, if we are not to starve. It is the duke who pays Leonardo for all the work he does.

There are paintings to be produced—and sculptures and entertainments for the palace—but that is not all. The duke needs to make sure that Milan is protected in case of attack, and it is part of Leonardo's work to find new ways of defending the city.

Leonardo says that men who go to war "are nothing but mad beasts"—and yet his ideas for war machines are beyond imagining. I have seen drawings for huge catapults, giant crossbows and battering rams, bridges that may be carried to wherever a river needs to be crossed, and cannon that fire from many barrels at once.

My favorite, though, is a design for what Leonardo calls "a covered chariot that is safe and cannot be assaulted." This looks a bit like a huge conical hat, big enough to carry eight soldiers and many cannon. It has wheels inside and is powered by cranks so that the soldiers may advance beneath it.

I like to look at these drawings and imagine what a battlefield might be like if all these amazing things were ever built and put to use. How noisy it would be under that chariot! The soldiers would surely be as deaf as adders by the time the battle was over. Perhaps Leonardo will have to invent a special helmet to protect their ears, too.

I'm amazed at how many drawings my master produces—dozens of sheets of paper covered in scores of intricate, detailed plans of real and imagined things.

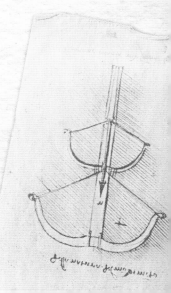

August 8, 1490

Leonardo is making more studies of birds and animals, cutting them open to see how their bones and muscles work. He appears very interested in how it is that birds can fly, and he has ideas for machines that might lift men up into the air! To think that we might someday join the birds—it scarcely seems possible.

But the workings of animals are not his only interest. I have also seen studies of human bodies—muscles and eyes and suchlike. How can my master have such knowledge? Does he secretly cut up men as well? I have heard rumors that he gets bodies from the morgue, but surely that can't be true?

My master will sometimes spend the morning out and about, observing doves or hawks fly, and then he'll return to the studio and examine the tiniest details of lifeless wings.

August 30, 1490

I have been allowed to do some more drawings and to listen in a little as Leonardo instructs the *garzoni* (the older apprentices). I am only a *discepolo* as yet—one who must fetch and carry for all the others—but I am learning more about the skills and techniques an artist needs, and today I learned two new words: *chiaroscuro* and *contrapposto*.

Chiaroscuro is the art of using light and shade to make any form that we draw look more solid and realistic. For example, if a mere circle is drawn in order to represent a globe, that circle could just as easily be something flat, like a coin. But by adding light and shade, we can show the roundness of the globe. I spent the morning practicing my chiaroscuro technique by drawing an apricot.

Contrapposto is my other new word. It means arranging the composition of figures in interesting poses so that their limbs point one way and their heads face in the opposite direction, I think.

We younger apprentices need to learn as much as we can from our master. When we progress to become garzoni, we'll be able to help with more skilled work such as painting backgrounds.

The purpose of such techniques, Leonardo said, is to make all that we do seem natural and real. I haven't had time to practice my contrapposto yet because in the afternoon I had to go back to my normal duties.

Leonardo was pleased with my drawing of an apricot, though, and he held it up to show the others.

"This is very good work for one who is only a *discepolo*," he said. "Paolo Valenti, you will become a *garzone* before we know it. Some of the older ones will have to look to their laurels."

This made me feel very proud, and I ignored Salaì later when he teased me.

September 7, 1490

More trouble with Salaì. Marco's silver drawing stylus has disappeared. Marco is one of the *garzoni*. Once again, Salaì swears he is innocent, but Carlo and I think different. Salaì has taken to sneaking out at night, climbing down the outside wall, and he often seems to have money in his pockets after his little excursions. We think he has taken the stylus and sold it. Sooner or later he will be found out, I am sure.

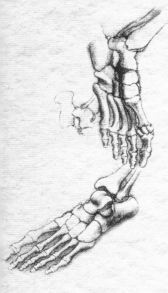

September 9, 1490

Yesterday morning I was looking at Leonardo's drawings of anatomy—human eyes, muscles, and bones—and marveling once again at his knowledge.

All of a sudden there was a voice at my shoulder. It was my master, asking whether these things were of interest to me. I said that they interested me very much but also baffled me. I wondered how he could know what lies beneath the skin.

"I will show you. Come with me this evening, Paolo, and you shall see what you shall see."

So the day passed, and then after supper, as the light was beginning to fail, Leonardo sent for me. He said that I should put on warm clothing, for it would be cold where we were going.

Cold? I began to wonder whether the rumors of Leonardo's trips to the morgue might be true after all, and the very thought made me shiver. As we hurried through the darkening streets of Milan, I could bear this thought no longer, and I asked if we were going to the morgue.

Leonardo laughed. "No, Paolo. We are going to the hospital. To the mortuary there. I have a physician friend who allows me to help him when he examines the bodies of the deceased. I am particularly interested in

Many people think it is wrong to cut up human bodies, but how else may we find out how the body works? It is not actually forbidden, but it's a good idea not to tell everyone about it.

criminals . . . what makes them as they are."

Morgue or hospital, there would be dead people there. I found that I wasn't looking forward to this visit half as much as my trip to the palace.

The hospital is huge. The building was dark when we arrived, and I was most nervous of entering. But I followed my master through the main gateway into an open moonlit square. It was surrounded by cloisters—pillared walkways that lay deep in shadow.

The sound of a man's voice in the darkness made me jump. A figure, tall and bearded, was waiting beside a pillar and called my master's name.

Leonardo greeted the man, whose name was Gianni, and thanked him for meeting us.

But the bearded man wanted to know who I was and why Leonardo had brought a boy with him. My master explained that I was an assistant, interested in watching him work.

"Interested he may be, Leonardo, but I cannot allow it. For you I can make an exception, but only for you. I can bring no children into the hospital. I am sorry. He must leave at once."

Leonardo thought this was a great pity, but he understood. He told me to wait for him at the hospital entrance instead and said he was sorry if I'd been disappointed.

Disappointed? I could have shaken that physician by the hand, I was so relieved. But I tried to look a little sorrowful and agreed that, yes, it was a shame.

The hospital cares for those who are gravely ill and cannot afford a doctor or even the apothecary's cures. Some patients are criminals with no family to bury them when they die. These are the bodies my master studies.

I sat on the darkened steps of the hospital entrance and waited. The air was warm, and in my jerkin I was warmer still. Perhaps I dozed off. At any rate, after a while I blinked to see that a group of figures had appeared on the other side of the street. Boys . . . four or five street urchins huddled together. They seemed to be having an argument, speaking in whispers that I could not hear. But gradually their voices rose, and their words became clear in the stillness of the night.

"How much for the silver stylus?"

"Ten *soldi*."

"Ten? I could buy a new one for eight, you little robber. I'll give you four."

"Agreed, then. Four *soldi*, and three for the shoes. That's seven *soldi*."

I'd heard that last speaker before. And as the boys shifted around into a different position, I recognized the figure of . . .

"Salaì!" My master's voice roared out, and I nearly fell down the steps from the shock of it. He was standing behind me, beneath the arch of the entrance, and must have heard everything.

I saw the white aghast faces of the boys all turn in our direction for a moment, and then they scattered, some running this way, some that. And with them went Salaì. Leonardo shouted after him again, but Salaì had gone.

"That thieving little devil!" My master was angry. Yet even so, perhaps not as furious as I would have expected. Leonardo gave me his drawings to carry, and he spoke not another word all the way home.

The night had almost gone by the time I got back to my chamber. Salaì was already in bed and pretending to be asleep, but I wasn't fooled. "I know you're awake, Salaì," I said. "You just wait till the morning—you'll be kicked out this time for certain."

September 10, 1490

Salaì is still here. I can't believe it. We all heard the roasting that Leonardo gave him, and the studio went quiet as we listened. Salaì was lazy . . . a glutton . . . an obstinate liar . . . an idle little thief . . . not worthy of the opportunity he had been given . . .

If I were to behave in this way, I would expect to be sent back to my father in disgrace. But poor Salaì has no family, and perhaps this has something to do with my master's kindness.

But Salaì wept and pleaded and begged not to be sent away. He promised to do better, and at the end of it all he is still with us. He came out of the side chamber, picked up his broom, and went about his duties as usual—and although he kept his head low for a while, it wasn't long before that silly little smile returned to his face. What can the master be thinking of to allow such behavior?

Later we spoke to Antonio about it— Carlo and I. We wanted to know why Salaì was being treated differently to the rest of us.

Antonio explained that Salaì is Leonardo's pet. He is like an orphaned puppy or a kitten and will never be thrown out into the street to starve no matter what mischief he gets into. And in time he will probably improve. Whether he will ever become an artist is another matter. But we other apprentices are taken more seriously, and we should think that a privilege.

November 3, 1490

Another visit to the palace! Once again I was entrusted with the task of carrying my master's drawings, and once again we found the duke eager to see what Leonardo had brought.

This time there were no angry words, only praise for Leonardo's designs. The duke particularly liked the war machines—in fact, he liked them so much that I wondered if he might start a war just to try them out.

The duke was also fascinated by Leonardo's drawings of anatomy. But here he chose his words a little more carefully.

"The pope does not approve of the carving up of human bodies, Leonardo," he said. "So I will not ask how you come by such detailed knowledge as this."

Leonardo said nothing, but he glanced briefly at me and winked.

Then came the best part of this visit. The duke noticed me and said to Leonardo, "And who is this boy you bring with you? Another *discepolo*?"

"The boy?" Leonardo stood upright. "That is Paolo Valenti—a talented youth. But he is not a mere *discepolo*. No, I think that perhaps from today he might call himself a *garzone*."

All eyes turned in my direction, and I thought my heart would burst with pride.

Leonardo showed a new drawing he calls Vitruvian Man. *It fascinates me—look how the man fits perfectly inside the circle and the square—and I could see it amazed the court ladies, too.*

December 2, 1490

Leonardo can play many musical instruments, but the lute is my favorite.

I no longer have to sweep the floors or run errands to the market—I leave that to Salaì. Instead, I practice my drawing and learn more each day about light and shade, pigment and perspective. I have even been allowed to do a little underpainting on some of the boards that are being prepared for scenery. The duke is planning to get married next year, and already Leonardo's designs for these celebrations are under way. How can all this be done? The duke is still anxious that work on the horse sculpture should continue. So what with this, the engineering works, the portrait commissions, the war machines, and all the inventions that come pouring from Leonardo's imagination, I think the studio will be busier than ever.

Today, for the first time, I heard my master playing the lute. A musician friend of his, Franchinus Gaffurius, had come to visit, and the two of them sat in the side chamber, working on some dancing music for the coming wedding. It sounded very beautiful, but that didn't surprise me. I believe that Leonardo can do anything he sets his mind to. He could probably fly if he wished.

Leonardo da Vinci. There can never be another like him. The rest of us can only shake our heads in wonder as we stumble along behind him, following in his footsteps as best we can.

May 10, 1498
Eight years later

Today I am back in Milan for a visit. I am now 18 years old; I finished my apprenticeship with Leonardo da Vinci a year or so ago and have set up my own small studio in Pavia. The town is alive with reports that Leonardo's great painting of the Last Supper is almost finished, and I thought I would come to see it for myself—if he will allow it. I made my way to the studio this afternoon. The master was not there, but many of the apprentices I spent the past few years with are still there, including that rascal Salaì. He is grown up now, too, and I doubt that he steals shoes anymore, but I also doubt whether he will ever gain renown as an artist.

In the studio, a wonderful thing happened. Seeing Salaì again brought to my mind the trouble he caused when he first arrived at the studio. It also made me recall the journal I once kept and how I used to hide it each night from his prying eyes. Could it still be there?

I went quietly to my old chamber, the room that I once shared with Carlo and Salaì, and lifted the loose floorboard—and there it was!

Nearly eight years it has been since I last saw this sheaf of papers or made any entry here. I don't remember why I stopped writing. Perhaps I was simply too busy for a while to bother with it and then never got around to starting again. And here it is, safe in my hands again! The paper has become discolored from damp, but the words are still perfectly readable. I wonder now at my younger self—the dreams I had then of becoming an artist and making my way in the world—and I feel proud that most of those dreams have come true.

After my long apprenticeship, I am a qualified master artist in my own right. I hope the fact that I was taught by the greatest, Leonardo da Vinci, will help me in my career.

Paolo, now aged 18

All the garzoni *in Leonardo's studio are busy making their own studies and sketches of the Last Supper scene, copying the master's studies for his great work.*

I asked Salaì if I could wait for Leonardo to return, and he shrugged his shoulders. "Do as you please. You might be waiting a long while, though. I can probably find you a broom if you get bored."

Same old Salaì, I thought. Always the clown. I wandered around the studio, marveling at some of Leonardo's new drawings. I asked Salaì where Leonardo might be found, and he said that the master would be searching the streets of Milan as usual. Searching for what? I wanted to know.

"Judas Iscariot," said Salaì. "He looks for one who has the face of Judas. For his painting of the Last Supper."

And then I understood. Leonardo often studied the faces of the ordinary citizens of Milan to use as models for his works— sometimes just sketching people in the street, sometimes bringing them into the studio. So now he sought one who would serve as his Judas—a villain or a rogue.

Leonardo did not return, and as it was growing late, I came back to my lodgings, bringing my journal with me to make these new entries. Tomorrow I shall try again to find my master.

May 11, 1498

I knew that Leonardo's painting of the Last Supper was in the monastery Santa Maria delle Grazie, but I hardly liked to enter there without invitation. It would be better to try to meet Leonardo at the studio if I could. I walked in that direction this morning and couldn't help smiling as I passed the apothecary's shop in Via Tiziano. I wondered whether the bad-tempered old apothecary was still there. As I peered through the window, I heard a familiar voice amid the noise and chatter of the busy street.

"Hmm. No. That face is too villainous even for Judas, I fear. A pity." I turned around, and there stood Leonardo da Vinci. It was my face he had been referring to!

He was carrying a drawing tablet and a silver stylus, still looking as outlandish as ever, his hair down to his shoulders. I bowed in greeting. Leonardo smiled and held out his hand. I told him how much I had been looking forward to meeting him again. He asked if things were going well for me, and I said yes indeed—I had a little studio in Pavia and had begun a small commission. But what of him and this great new painting that all were talking about?

"The Last Supper? Yes, the major part of it is done—thanks be. The prior complains to Ludovico at the lack of progress, and Ludovico complains to me. They are like two old women nagging at me, and I get no peace from either. I have explained to both that I work on the Last Supper for at least two hours every day, but neither understands that such work may consist of thinking as much as painting. But there. Those that hold the purse strings look only for the finished result and have little interest in the process. Would you like to see it?"

This was what I had hoped for all along, the very purpose of my visit, and so of course I said yes.

The Last Supper story tells of the last meal that Jesus Christ shared with his disciples, or followers, before his death. Judas, who was soon to betray him, was at the meal.

On the way to the monastery, Leonardo told me of his search for Judas. He explained that, for him, it is always better to find a real face than to dream one up. But Judas Iscariot was a difficult one to find. Leonardo said that he had been waiting for a Judas to appear for more than a year now. He has even told the duke that if he can find no better, he might have to use the face of the prior himself. I laughed at this—I wonder if the duke did, too. I asked if the difficulty of the search meant that the streets of Milan were full of such good, innocent people that no villain could be found. Leonardo said that there were villains enough in this city, but he looks for one in a million, not just one in ten.

As we entered the grand building, Santa Maria delle Grazie, Leonardo told me that the Last Supper is on the wall of the refectory, or dining room, where the monks sit to eat their own supper. It seemed appropriate.

The painting is breathtaking, an astonishing piece of work. I wondered first at the huge scale of it—it's longer than four men lying head to toe and nearly as high as three standing upon one another's shoulders. And then there's the composition and perspective—the eye being drawn to the central figure of Jesus, with his disciples at the table on either side of him. Each of the men might have stepped from our own streets, so real and human are their faces. Only Judas remains blank. But the colors! How had Leonardo managed to achieve such brilliance?

"It's a new technique of my own devising," he said. "I've used tempera mixed with a very small amount of linseed oil and painted that onto a layer of gesso rather than wet plaster. The linseed oil means that it doesn't dry as quickly, so I am able to work on my figures with more care. What do you think?"

I said that I thought I might do better to lay down my brushes and take to shoe mending like my father after all.

"Ha! My old tutor, Andrea del Verrocchio, once said something similar. You're very kind. But come. Standing here idle will not do. We are busy men, both of us."

I could have stood there idle all day and not guessed the hours wasted, but I followed the master out into the sunlight once more. Leonardo said he hoped I would

come to see him again, for he will always find time for his best students. That Leonardo da Vinci considered me one of his best students was praise indeed, and I felt very proud as we shook hands in farewell.

Now I must return to Pavia, to my own work—inspired as always to try harder, do better, live up to the standard that the master sets. If ever I should lose patience, I have only to think of Leonardo, walking the streets of Milan for a year, searching for that one face in a million: Judas Iscariot.

It is amazing—the painting looks like an extension of this very room, as if the Last Supper were taking place right here in front of us.

What Happened Next?

Later in 1498, Leonardo finished work on *The Last Supper*. It is said that in the end he used the prior of the monastery, a man he had come to see as aggressive and troublesome, as his model for Judas. The duke had once laughed heartily at this suggestion, and like the rest of Milan, he was delighted with Leonardo's finished masterpiece. He gave Leonardo his own vineyard near the monastery as part of his payment for the work.

Before long, however, life in Milan began to change dramatically. Leonardo's magnificent painting was not the only talk of the town. Citizens' attention was turning from the quiet of the monastery to the heat and noise of battle as the threat of war approached the city.

War had raged throughout the Italian peninsula just a few years earlier, in 1494. Then, the French king, Charles VIII, led a swift, brutal, and terrifying invasion. Milan, with Duke Ludovico Sforza in charge, actually encouraged the invasion at first, joining with its old ally France against Naples. But as the fighting wore on, neighboring Italian city-states also suffered brutal attacks by the French. Ludovico switched sides and helped form a new Italian alliance—the League of Venice—to defeat France.

The French were beaten in 1495. But in the summer of 1499, French armies were moving through Italy again. This time, Duke Ludovico Sforza found himself without the support of powerful allies and vulnerable to attack. The new French king, Louis XII, had a minor claim to the throne of Milan. Leonardo's elaborate war machines still existed only as drawings and ideas—they had never been built. Milan was in real danger.

One after another, important towns not far from Milan were seized, without much difficulty, by Louis's armies. Ludovico had lost money, some of his armies, and even the support of some of the city's people. He fled Milan. In September, the chaos of war arrived at last as hundreds of French soldiers poured through the city walls. King Louis himself rode into the city. He promised the people of Milan that he would free them from high taxes, and he soon took control of the city.

The clattering of horses' hooves and the shouts of French soldiers brought noise and chaos to Milan's streets. The French took control of the city quickly, without a great deal of violence.

Duke Ludovico Sforza had left Milan and was living in exile in the nearby city of Novara.

The French soldiers wasted no time in seizing the Sforza palace, which Ludovico and his family had fled in such a hurry. There was no real fighting, but it must have been a frightening time as the soldiers made their presence felt, looting businesses, attacking, and even killing people. Leonardo had to think of his own safety and livelihood. How could he survive without his patron, and who would commission paintings and statues in a time of war?

One of Leonardo's creations, the clay model for his magnificent horse monument, was found by the soldiers, standing in a vineyard near the monastery of Santa Maria delle Grazie. The plan to cast it in bronze had long been abandoned—in 1495, the duke had sent the bronze to his father-in-law in Ferrara to be made into cannon for defense against the French—and the clay model was all that remained of Leonardo's once-great project. The French archers and crossbowmen used it as target practice, firing their arrows at its huge lifelike body until it was smashed to smithereens.

Leonardo left Milan along with his friend Luca Paoli, who had been the duke's court mathematician, and Salaì, who was still living with Leonardo as his assistant.

LEAVING MILAN

Leonardo decided it was time to leave Milan. Sensibly, before the French had taken control of the city in December 1499, he had arranged for 600 ducats, a good sum of money, to be sent to a bank account that he held in Florence. Not long afterward, he packed up his belongings and left the city. Once again, Leonardo was offering his services as a painter, sculptor, military inventor, and engineer, just as he had when he wrote to Duke Ludovico Sforza all those years before.

In 1500, the French laid siege to Novara. Ludovico was handed over and kept as a prisoner until his death in 1508. The French ruled Milan until 1513, when Ludovico's son Massimiliano Sforza was allowed to return as duke.

Leonardo settled in Florence in 1500. In the years that followed, he lived and worked in Florence, Milan again, and Rome. His many, varied projects included magnificent religious paintings and portraits, brilliant ideas for war machines and other engineering projects, and more studies of the human body. In 1516, he became the official painter and engineer to the French king Francis I. He remained in France until his death, at the age of 67, in 1519.

And what of the masterpiece of Leonardo and Ludovico's partnership, *The Last Supper*, one of the most remarkable paintings of the Renaissance? By 1517, only a few years after it was finished, it was already badly damaged. The wall on which it was painted was of poor quality, and changes in temperature or moisture had made the plaster start to crumble away. Soon the faces he had worked so hard to perfect were almost invisible. It has now been painstakingly restored, however, and can be seen in Milan's Santa Maria delle Grazie.

Leonardo's Story

Leonardo was born on April 15, 1452, in the countryside near the small town of Vinci in the republic of Florence. His father, Ser Piero, was a notary (a type of lawyer), and his mother, Caterina, was a peasant girl. Leonardo's parents were not married—in fact, Ser Piero married a wealthy lady from Florence soon after Leonardo's birth. Leonardo spent much of his childhood in Vinci with his mother, grandparents, uncle, half sisters, and half brother.

Ser Piero made sure that Leonardo learned how to read and write and that he gained some knowledge of Latin grammar and mathematics. At the age of ten or 11, Leonardo was taken to Florence, where his father found him a position as an apprentice to Andrea del Verrocchio, one of the city's most respected artists. By the time he finished his apprenticeship, Leonardo was becoming a brilliant painter.

For the next 40 years or so, Leonardo worked in Florence, Milan, and Rome—as an artist, scientist, engineer, and inventor for some of the most important figures of the time. Some of the events of his life are illustrated opposite.

Paolo's world

In our story, Paolo is an imaginary character, but many of the people he writes about in his diary were real. Antonio (Giovanni Antonio Boltraffio), for example, was Leonardo's chief assistant for several years and later an artist in his own right. And, as the story says, Leonardo always looked after the rascal Salaì (Gian Giacomo Caprotti di Oreno). He grew up to be Leonardo's lifelong friend, servant, and assistant, staying in his household until Leonardo's death.

1452 *Leonardo is born close to the town of Vinci in the countryside near Florence.*

1466–1469 *Leonardo moves to Florence and becomes an apprentice in the studio of Andrea del Verrocchio.*

1490 *Leonardo works on the Sforza horse and draws the Vitruvian Man, among other things. Salaì joins the studio as an apprentice.*

1497 *Work on The Last Supper is under way.*

1503 *Leonardo begins work on his most famous painting, the Mona Lisa. In 1506–1513, he is back in Milan—the city is now ruled by the French.*

1513 *Leonardo moves to Rome, where he lives and works at the Vatican court (the pope's headquarters).*

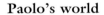

1472 *Leonardo paints one of the angels in Verrocchio's painting* The Baptism of Christ. *He also finishes his apprenticeship, becoming a master artist and a member of Florence's Guild of Saint Luke.*

1481 *Leonardo leaves Florence for Milan, where he finds work at the court of Duke Ludovico Sforza.*

1498 *Ludovico Sforza gives Leonardo a vineyard in Milan. But there is not much time for him to enjoy it, as in the fall of* **1499**, *French troops invade the city and Leonardo leaves.*

1500–1505 *Leonardo works in Florence again, along with his great rival, the artist and sculptor Michelangelo.*

1516 *Leonardo moves to France to work for the king, Francis I. Salaì is one of his companions. In* **1519**, *Leonardo dies, at the age of 67, in Amboise, France.*

Important events in Europe

1400

1420 Filippo Brunelleschi builds the dome of Florence Cathedral.
1434 Cosimo de' Medici becomes the first Medici ruler of Florence.

1450

1453 End of Hundred Years' War between France and England. Ottoman Turks capture Constantinople (now Istanbul, Turkey), bringing about the collapse of the Byzantine Empire.
1455 Johann Gutenberg produces the first printed book in Europe, a Bible.
1476 Seven-year-old Gian Galeazzo Sforza becomes duke of Milan, and his uncle Ludovico Sforza soon takes charge as the city's real ruler.
1479 Ferdinand of Aragon and Isabella of Castile begin their joint rule as the "Catholic kings" of a powerful Spain.
1484–1486 Plague sweeps Milan and wipes out one-third of its population.
1492 Explorer Christopher Columbus reaches the New World.
1494 Wars in Italy begin.
1499 The French invade Milan, Duke Ludovico Sforza flees, and the city is brought under French rule.

1500

1501–1504 Michelangelo makes his sculpture of David.
1508–1512 Michelangelo paints the ceiling of the Sistine Chapel in Rome.
1517 Martin Luther nails his 95 theses to the door of a church in Wittenberg (in modern-day Germany), sparking the Protestant Reformation.
1519 Charles V becomes the Holy Roman emperor and the most powerful ruler in Europe.

1529 Siege of Vienna: Ottoman armies' failure to take the city means that their advance through central Europe comes to a halt.

1543 Nicolaus Copernicus publishes his theory that Earth moves around the Sun.

1550

1558 Elizabeth I becomes the queen of England.

THE HEART OF EUROPE

Leonardo da Vinci was born in a village that was part of the city-state of Florence in northern Italy. This small corner of Europe was the heart of the continent. It had the biggest, wealthiest cities—busy trade centers where art and culture flourished.

Fifteenth-century Europe was not made up of all the countries we know today. France, Portugal, England, and Hungary were independent nations, but there were also hundreds of small territories. Much of Europe was part of the Holy Roman Empire, a union of many kingdoms, duchies, and republics. Spain, once several kingdoms, was just emerging as a single powerful nation with growing influence in Europe and beyond.

Italy was not one country as it is today but a collection of city-states. Milan and Turin were duchies, ruled by dukes. Venice, Florence, and Genoa were republics, ruled not by a duke, prince, or king but by councils elected by the citizens. There were the Papal States—areas controlled by the pope from Rome—and the kingdom of Naples in the south. Rivalry between Italy's city-states sometimes turned into war. But there was enough peace and stability to allow the cities to grow and prosper.

ENGLAND

London ●

FRANCE   Paris ●

Amboise ●

Leonardo spent his last years in Amboise.

The palace in Segovia was one of many fine fortress palaces in Spain.

PORTUGAL

● Madrid   Aragon

Castile

SPAIN

Granada

From the 1480s onward, explorers from Europe sailed the Atlantic Ocean in search of trade, wealth, and new lands to conquer.

The towns of Flanders grew rich by trading wool cloth.

Antwerp

Mainz

The first European printing shop opened in the German city of Mainz in 1455.

HOLY ROMAN EMPIRE

Turin

Milan

Pavia

Genoa

Venice

Bologna

Florence

Rome

Naples

HUNGARY

The areas shown in color on this map are the Italian city-states.

OTTOMAN EMPIRE

Constantinople (Istanbul)

In 1453, the Ottomans captured Constantinople and made it their capital city.

*In this map of the **city of Milan**, you can see the heavily fortified city walls, the impressive Sforza palace (at the top of the picture), and the cathedral (in the center of the picture), which was still a construction site when Leonardo lived there.*

Milan

The duchy of Milan, where Paolo's story is set, had been one of Italy's most powerful city-states for a long time. The city was well known for its military strength, culture, and wealth. Its craftsmen were skilled in military engineering, and Milanese smiths were famous for the quality of their metalwork, from impressive armor to elaborate, finely decorated locks and keys.

The Sforza family had been Milan's rulers since 1450. At the time of our story, in 1490, the young Gian Galeazzo Sforza was the duke of Milan, but the real ruler was his uncle, Leonardo's patron Ludovico Sforza, who was the duke of Bari. In 1494, Gian Galeazzo died and Ludovico officially became the duke of Milan. Many people believed that he poisoned his nephew so that he could seize power.

THE RENAISSANCE

Leonardo da Vinci was alive during an exciting time. The 1300s had been a period of great hardship—there were wars, famines, and revolts, and the Black Death killed more than one-third of Europe's people. By the 1450s, things were changing. There was a flourishing of art, culture, and science, which later came to be known as the Renaissance, meaning "rebirth." Northern Italy was at its heart.

New ideas

The Renaissance saw the rebirth of ideas and knowledge from ancient Greece and Rome—ideas that had long been ignored or forgotten in Europe—combined with new thinking about religion and exciting advances in science. A fascination with learning took hold in Europe's cities. Trade with powerful empires outside Europe was growing, and through it came learning from the Chinese and Arabs, who were far ahead of Europe in science and technology at this time.

Art and science

Before the Renaissance, the church had dominated learning and the arts. Scholars and artists alike concentrated on studying the Bible and thinking about how people could get to heaven. Now, they started to focus more on human life and the world around them. Painters and sculptors made figures much more lifelike and realistic than ever before. Religious themes were still very important, but even then, the people looked like they were really human. Leonardo went to great effort to make sure that the figures he painted in *The Last Supper* were based on real faces he saw in Milan, for example.

The Renaissance eagerness to understand the world went far beyond art. It was a time of great advances in mathematics, astronomy, medicine, science, and technology, too. One of the most important machines ever invented, the printing press, was developed at this time.

The city of Florence was one of the centers of the Renaissance. Architect Filippo Brunelleschi (1377–1446) designed many of its buildings. He figured out how to construct the cathedral's huge dome, which, at 270 ft. (82m) high, was the highest dome anyone had ever built.

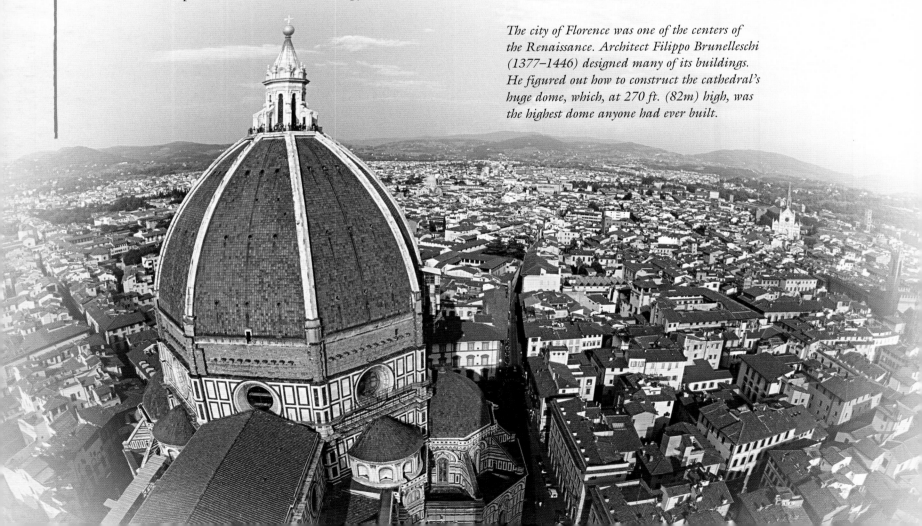

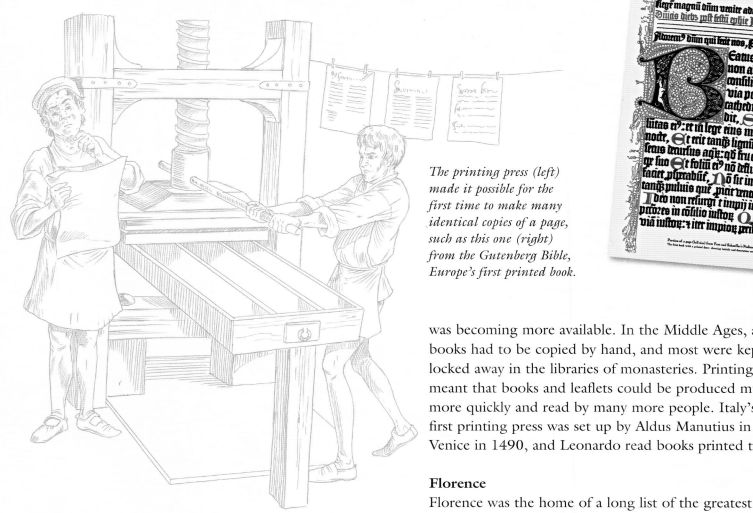

The printing press (left) made it possible for the first time to make many identical copies of a page, such as this one (right) from the Gutenberg Bible, Europe's first printed book.

was becoming more available. In the Middle Ages, all books had to be copied by hand, and most were kept locked away in the libraries of monasteries. Printing meant that books and leaflets could be produced much more quickly and read by many more people. Italy's first printing press was set up by Aldus Manutius in Venice in 1490, and Leonardo read books printed there.

Florence

Florence was the home of a long list of the greatest artists of the time: in addition to Leonardo da Vinci, there had been Giotto, Paolo Uccello, Piero della Francesca, Sandro Botticelli, Raphael, Michelangelo, and the architect Filippo Brunelleschi. Brunelleschi studied mathematics and examined the ruins of Roman buildings and used what he learned to come up with a new architectural style. The wealthy families of Florence, especially the ruling Medici family, encouraged great artists to work in the city, so Florence produced some of the most famous works of Renaissance art.

This is the emblem of the Medici family, who ruled Florence from 1469. The circles on the emblem might represent coins, showing that they were bankers.

Why Italy?

Italy was a collection of city-states. Many were very wealthy—rich trading centers peopled with well-to-do merchants and bankers, skilled craftsmen, and educated people—and ruled by super-rich families. The combination of wealth, skill, and learning meant that there was the money to pay for great art and the people to create it. Rich families paid for new palaces and public buildings and hired artists to paint their portraits and create impressive sculptures. Rulers wanted the best and the brightest people—like Leonardo da Vinci—working for them.

Everyday life

Life was still tough in Italy's cities. There was always the threat of war and disease, for rich and poor alike. There were many outbreaks of plague—one swept Milan in 1484–1486. But some things were improving. Most people could not read, but for those who could, learning

PEOPLE AND POWER

Even today, we refer to someone who excels at everything as a Renaissance man or Renaissance woman. During the 1400s and 1500s, the ideal person, or "universal man," was expected to be a brilliant scholar, excelling at all the arts and sciences and speaking several languages. He should also have been a fine swordsman and horseman, witty, a skilled musician, and a responsible citizen.

Princes and countries

This was a time when European kings and princes had enormous wealth and strength. The great powers in the 1400s and 1500s were Spain, France, and the Holy Roman Empire. England was rising in importance. The Italian states and their rulers had their roles, too. The pope himself was a prince, ruler of the Papal States, as well as the head of the Roman Catholic Church. There was also the ever-growing Ottoman Empire to the east, a Muslim Turkish empire both respected and feared by its Christian European neighbors.

Elizabeth I (1536–1603) was the queen of England for more than 40 years. Like many Renaissance princesses, she was exceptionally well educated and could read and write Latin, Greek, French, Spanish, and Italian. In this portrait, painted after her navy had defeated the Spanish Armada, she holds a globe to represent her power.

Charles V (1500–1558, left) became king of Spain in 1516 and within three years was also the Holy Roman emperor. This made him the head of the largest empire since that of ancient Rome, and by far the most powerful ruler in Europe. Other rulers always wanted to stay on the right side of him—or, on the other hand, to attack and outdo him. His empire grew and grew as Spain conquered lands in the Americas, but such a large realm meant there was always an invasion or revolt somewhere. He was the grandson of Ferdinand and Isabella (see page 53, opposite).

Francis I of France (1494–1547, right) was another contender for the title of most powerful ruler in Europe—in fact, he tried to become Holy Roman emperor instead of Charles V. He was a fine soldier and scholar. He expanded his royal library and was an admirer of Italian art, inviting Leonardo da Vinci to be his official painter.

Holding on to power

European rulers may have been powerful, but their power was never safe, as it depended on success in battle, good health, and the ability to produce heirs, among other things. Princes needed to display their importance and show that they were cultured, intelligent Renaissance men as well as fearsome military leaders. No ruler could feel safe from being overthrown, and they often needed to be ruthless and brutal to succeed.

Suleiman I (1494–1566), known as "the Magnificent" and "the Lawgiver," was the Ottoman sultan (emperor). The growth of his empire sent shock waves throughout Europe, and European leaders tried and failed to form a grand alliance against him. He inspired a golden age of art and learning at his own court and rebuilt much of his capital city, Constantinople (Istanbul).

Ferdinand and Isabella

Christopher Columbus

Niccolò Machiavelli (1469–1527), a politician in Florence, knew all about princes and power. His book The Prince advised rulers to do anything, however ruthless, to hold on to power and keep peace. He wrote, "It is much safer for a prince to be feared than loved."

Ferdinand of Aragon (1452–1516) and *Isabella of Castile* (1451–1504) were tough monarchs who united their kingdoms and went on to bring the rest of Spain under their rule. They sponsored the Italian-born explorer *Christopher Columbus* (1451–1506), who discovered new lands in the Americas in 1492. Soon, much of the Americas were part of Spain's huge empire.

IDEAS AND INVENTIONS

Renaissance artists and scholars worked eagerly to expand human knowledge. There were great achievements and inventions in mathematics, astronomy, art, and technology. In fact, art and science were not thought of as different subjects as they often are today but as part of the same thirst for discovery. Leonardo thought of himself as a scientist, inventor, engineer, and musician as well as a painter.

The human body

Leonardo wanted to understand and illustrate the body's inner workings. To do this he needed to dissect (cut up) dead bodies. This had rarely been done before, as the church taught that it was disrespectful to God, and people felt uneasy about it. But things were changing, and during his lifetime, Leonardo dissected up to 30 bodies.

His studies of muscles, bones, joints, and organs are amazingly detailed, and he figured out the structure of the heart and its system of blood vessels. He did not quite understand how it worked, but his conclusions were the most accurate of any that had ever been made on the subject. His studies were not made public, however, and not until the mid-1500s did others begin to match or improve upon his discoveries.

This telescope is a copy of the one developed by Italian scientist Galileo Galilei (1564–1642). With this new invention, Galileo studied planets and moons and showed that the planet Venus moves around the Sun, not Earth. Copernicus's illustration (above left) also shows Earth and other planets revolving around the central Sun.

Discoveries in astronomy

Renaissance scientists changed the way people understand the universe. For centuries, European thought (and church teaching) had been based on the theory that Earth was at the center of the universe, with the Sun and planets moving around it. In 1543, Polish astronomer Nicolaus Copernicus (1473–1543) came up with a new theory—that the Sun is at the center and Earth is just one of the planets orbiting it. Before Copernicus's discovery, Leonardo observed the changing appearance of the Moon and concluded that it does not shine with its own light but reflects light from the Sun.

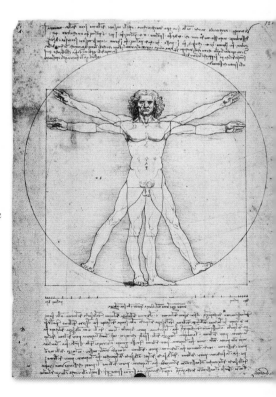

*Leonardo examined the mathematical shapes and proportions of things. In this drawing, **Vitruvian Man** (1490), Leonardo looked at the human body in this way. How large was his head in proportion to his body, and how long should his arms and legs be? The drawing showed that the arms and legs of the human figure could fit inside both a circle and a square, depending on how the figure was arranged.*

A modern model based on Leonardo's plans for a flying machine. This machine has flapping wings like a bird's. The pilot drives it with his legs.

Flying machines

The question of how birds fly fascinated Leonardo. He observed birds in flight and dissected their wings. He believed that the laws of science meant it must be possible for humans to fly and came up with several designs for flying machines. They included a simple parachute, a machine with flapping wings, a type of airplane, and an "airscrew," which many people consider to be the earliest design for a helicopter. We know of none that were successfully built in Leonardo's time— although he probably made some models and attempts at flight, and he kept on developing better ideas and approaches to the problem. Modern models based on his glider designs have been made recently, and they do work.

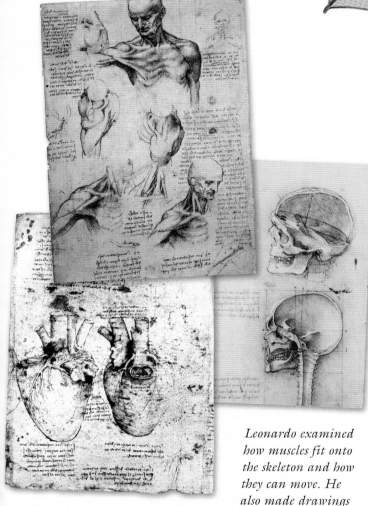

Leonardo examined how muscles fit onto the skeleton and how they can move. He also made drawings of human skulls. In the 1500s, he studied the workings of the heart, examining and drawing ox hearts, like the one above, as well as human ones.

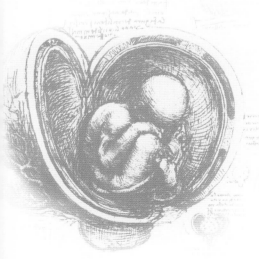

Leonardo made this detailed study of a baby in the uterus (womb) in 1512. Earlier studies of animals would have helped him learn how a baby develops inside its mother.

With this propeller (airscrew) (drawing c. 1489), Leonardo considered that one way to lift an object into the air would be to use a spiral screw to create vertical lift. Leonardo's notes gave no clue to how it would be powered, but the idea is used in helicopters today.

LIFE AS AN ARTIST

the emblem of Florence's guild of stonemasons and carpenters

Like all skilled craftsmen in the 1400s, artists spent many years training to learn their craft. Most painters would work to standard patterns and would not sign their work or become recognized in their own right. However, there were many exceptions to this rule, as the Renaissance saw dozens of brilliant and renowned artists.

Guilds and patrons

All craftsmen needed a license to work, and to get this they had to belong to a guild, an organization that controlled each profession's trade and standards. Then they needed to make sure that they had enough work and money to survive. Many artists relied on wealthy patrons for this. Patrons might give an artist large individual commissions or pay him a regular salary to cover the everyday costs of living and keeping a studio or workshop open. Duke Ludovico Sforza was Leonardo's patron in Milan, for example.

Italy's rulers competed to be the best artists' patrons. Here, Lorenzo de' Medici (ruler of Florence 1469–1492), surrounded by artists, admires a sculpture by Michelangelo.

Apprentices would grind up materials including minerals, plants, and even beetles. These dull-looking substances could make bright-colored pigments.

Life as an apprentice

A boy would become an apprentice at the age of ten or so, leaving his family and going to live with his employer. Almost all apprentices were boys. To start with, an artist's apprentice would sweep floors, run errands, polish marble, and build scaffolding. He would learn to make paints by grinding pigments into powder and mixing them with egg yolk or oil, and to make paintbrushes by tying animal hair to wooden handles. He would prepare wooden panels for painting by boiling them and coating them with clear glue and a substance called gesso. He would also study drawing. Apprenticeships lasted seven years or more: as the years went on, an apprentice would help with the paintings, filling in background landscapes and details such as clothing and hair. Finally—a little like passing a test—he had to produce a piece of work called a masterwork. Then he was qualified to join a guild and work as an artist in his own right.

Leonardo the apprentice

Leonardo da Vinci began his apprenticeship, with Andrea del Verrocchio in Florence, around 1464. Verrocchio was a sculptor, painter, and goldsmith, and his studio produced all kinds of work. It was a great place for a talented boy such as Leonardo to learn his craft. As the years went on, he began to help with major works. He is generally believed to have painted one of the angels in Verrocchio's *Baptism of Christ*, just before he completed his apprenticeship, around 1472. At the same time, he was working on his own masterwork, *The Annunciation* (see page 58). There is even a story that Verrocchio was so amazed at the quality of his student's work that he decided he never wanted to paint again!

Botticelli's **La Primavera** *(Spring, c. 1482) shows springtime in the garden of Venus (center), the Roman goddess of love. Renaissance painters often portrayed scenes of Greek or Roman gods.*

New techniques

Renaissance artists made sure that their paintings and sculptures were composed in mathematically perfect proportions. They used perspective well (perspective gives the illusion of space and distance to a flat painting). At the same time they were developing new materials and techniques. Instead of using tempera, a sticky paint made from pigment mixed with egg yolk, which dries hard very quickly, artists started to try mixing pigments with oil to make oil paint, which dries much more slowly and gives very rich, glowing colors.

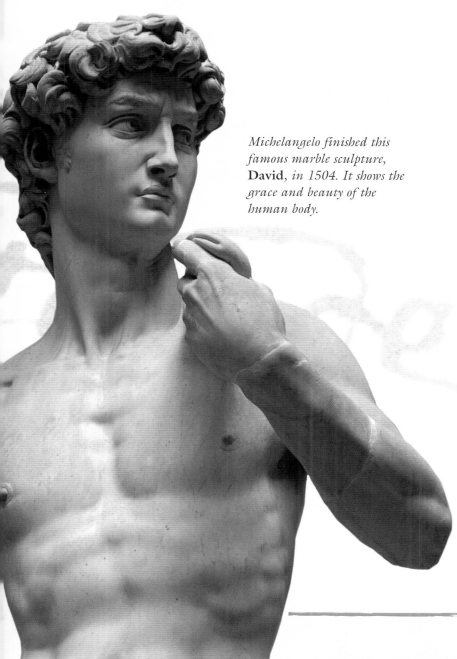

Michelangelo finished this famous marble sculpture, **David**, *in 1504. It shows the grace and beauty of the human body.*

Renaissance rivals

Leonardo met many other important artists during his career. Perhaps the greatest of these, Michelangelo Buonarroti (1475–1564) became Leonardo's biggest rival. They first met in Florence around 1500. Michelangelo mocked Leonardo about the horse statue that he had failed to finish in Milan, and Leonardo was deeply hurt. The unfriendly rivalry between him and Michelangelo became well known. The two were commissioned to paint important murals in Florence in 1503 (see page 59), but neither completed their work. In 1505, Michelangelo moved to Rome, where he painted the ceiling of the Sistine Chapel—one of the highlights of Renaissance art.

There were many other major Italian artists working around the same time as Leonardo da Vinci, including:

Sandro Botticelli (1445–1510) was a student in Verrocchio's workshop at the same time as Leonardo.

Giotto (c. 1267–1337) lived a long time before Leonardo and is often regarded as the founder of modern painting.

Piero della Francesca (c. 1415–1492) was fascinated by geometry and painted serene, mathematically perfect works.

Raphael (1483–1520) worked with Leonardo and Michelangelo in Florence. He went on to become one of the greatest and most prolific artists of the Renaissance.

LEONARDO'S FAMOUS PAINTINGS

In **Lady with an Ermine** *(c. 1489–1490, left), a portrait of Cecilia Gallerani, Leonardo captured a bright sparkle in this intelligent woman's face, as well as showing the rich colors of her clothes.* **The Annunciation** *(1472–1473, above) was painted when Leonardo was only a little over 20 years old. The details, such as the white flowers held by the angel, are very fine.*

Leonardo was one of the best artists of all time, and we know that he produced a huge amount of work. He completed only a relatively small number of paintings, but they are magnificent and inspiring.

Leonardo's masterwork was completed around 1472–1473. *The Annunciation* shows the Biblical story of the angel Gabriel appearing to Mary to tell her that God has chosen her to be the mother of Jesus Christ. Leonardo brought an impressive combination of calm and emotion to the scene. From this first major painting onward, he continued to improve and develop, experimenting with materials and inventing techniques, with some astonishing results.

Popular subjects

The most popular subjects commissioned in Leonardo's time were personal portraits for the wealthy and religious scenes to adorn new cathedrals and palaces. Leonardo excelled at both. His human figures were very well drawn, and he was praised for giving a sense of life to the figures so that they seemed full of motion and energy.

In Milan

Leonardo's Milan court portraits included *Lady with an Ermine, Portrait of a Lady,* and *Portrait of a Musician,* his only known painted portrait of a man. Religious works included *The Virgin of the Rocks,* the *Madonna Litta,* and, of course, *The Last Supper.* This was the greatest of his works from his years at Duke Ludovico's court, a magnificent finishing touch to the new monastery—and one of the great masterpieces of the Renaissance.

The famous *Mona Lisa*

In 1503, Leonardo began work on a portrait of a seated woman. Experts agree that she is Lisa Gherardini del Giocondo, the wife of a Florence silk merchant, and "Mona Lisa" is short for Madonna Lisa (Italian for "Madam Lisa"). Another name for the painting is *La Gioconda*, meaning "the amused one." This word refers to her expression, and it is also her name, as it is the feminine form of Giocondo. There are other theories, however, and a sense of mystery surrounds her identity. Some people think she could be the Renaissance princess Isabella d'Este.

In 1503, the same year as he started the Mona Lisa, *Leonardo began another huge project. With his rival Michelangelo, he was asked by the city council of Florence to produce two huge wall paintings for the council chamber. Leonardo's painting was to show the Battle of Anghiari, a famous victory by Florence over Milan. In the end, however, the paintings were abandoned. All that survives are some sketch studies and this copy (above) done partially by Flemish painter Peter Paul Rubens.*

The finished painting was never delivered to the sitter. Leonardo probably kept it in his studio to show visitors. He took it with him to France, and it was among paintings he left to Salaì when he died. The story doesn't end there: King Francis I soon bought it to display in his palace. In 1800, the French emperor Napoleon loved it so much that he moved it to his bedroom. Today, more than 500 years after Leonardo began work, this painting is probably the most famous in the world. Around six million visitors every year flock to the Musée du Louvre in Paris, France, to admire it.

The composition of **Mona Lisa** *is traditional for a Renaissance portrait, but there is something very special about the painting. Leonardo used his own new technique, called sfumato ("smoky"), in which a buildup of thin, almost translucent layers of oil paint softens the painting's lines and edges. The landscape looks misty and atmospheric. The figure is beautifully executed and her clothing—at first glance just a simple dark dress—is very finely detailed. Her expression is mysterious as she gazes at something just to the right of the viewer.*

GLOSSARY

alliance
A group of people or countries that have made an agreement to work or fight together.

anatomy
The study of the structure of the body.

apothecary
A person licensed to sell medicines; equivalent to a pharmacist today.

apprentice
A young person learning a trade from a skilled master.

architect
Someone who designs buildings.

astronomy
The study of the stars and planets and the wider universe.

battering ram
A type of weapon—a large beam used for knocking down walls and doors.

catapult
A type of weapon—a device for launching an arrow or cannonball without any explosives.

cathedral
A large important church.

cherubim
The plural of cherub—a type of angel, often depicted in painting and sculpture as a sweet-looking child.

chiaroscuro
The word for the art of using light and shade in a drawing or painting. It is one way of making objects appear more realistic.

citizen
An inhabitant of a city.

city-state
A small, independent country based around a large town or city.

commission
A piece of work, especially painting, sculpture, or building work, that is ordered before it is made.

composition
How items in a painting are arranged to make a satisfactory whole.

contrapposto
A way of showing figures in a painting, with parts of the body twisted in different directions. For example, a figure may be shown with legs facing one way and chest and shoulders turned to face the other way.

court
The place where a royal ruler (for example, a king, queen, or duke) lives and conducts official business.

crossbow
A type of weapon used for shooting bolts.

***discepolo* (plural: *discepoli*)**
The Italian word for an apprentice, especially one at the beginning of his studies.

dissect
To cut up something for the purpose of examining or studying it.

empire
A group of countries ruled by another country.

engineer
Someone who uses scientific knowledge to solve practical problems (for example, by designing or building machines).

ermine
A small furry animal—also called a stoat—or its fur.

exile
Living away from one's home country, not out of choice but because it is not safe to stay at home.

***garzone* (plural: *garzoni*)**
The Italian word for an apprentice, especially an artist's apprentice.

gesso
A substance made from white chalk, glue, and water used to coat wooden panels in order to make a smooth surface on which to paint.

guild
A trade association of craftsmen, bankers, or merchants, responsible for standards of work.

heir
A person who is entitled to money, possessions, or position when someone else dies. The heir to a throne is the person who will become the next ruler when the current ruler dies.

inventor
Someone who creates or discovers new things or new ways of doing things.

linseed oil
The oil from flaxseeds which is used to make oil paint.

masterwork
A very good piece of work produced by an apprentice at the end of his training.

monastery
A religious community of monks and the building in which they live and work.

Moorish
Having to do with the Moors, a people originally from Morocco who controlled most of Spain from the A.D. 700s–1400s.

morgue or **mortuary**
A place where dead bodies are kept. They can be names for the same thing, but in Paolo's story, they are different places. The morgue he fears is the main city morgue, full of bodies waiting to be buried. The hospital mortuary is much smaller and, to him, slightly less frightening.

mortar and pestle
A tool (the pestle) made of hard wood or stone that is used with a bowl (the mortar) to crush or grind items into a powder.

Ottoman Empire
The lands ruled by the Ottomans, a Turkish people; by the mid-1500s, the most powerful empire in Europe and the Middle East.

patron
A wealthy person who commissions and pays for a work of art or who pays an artist a salary.

peninsula
A strip of land jutting out into the ocean.

perspective
A way of drawing three-dimensional objects on a flat surface to create a sense of depth and distance.

physician
Another word for a doctor.

pigment
Colored powder used to make paint. Pigments can come from plants, animals, and minerals.

pope
The head of the Catholic Church, based in Rome. During the 1400s, the pope was also the ruler of the Papal States.

portrait
A picture of a real person.

prior
A monastery's chief monk.

proportion
The mathematical relationship between the size of an object and the size of its parts.

refectory
A communal dining room.

Renaissance
The period of European history, from around the 1300s–1600s, when many advances in art, science, and technology were made.

republic
A country that is ruled by representatives of its people, not by a king, queen, or duke. Florence and Venice were important republics in the 1400s.

ruthless
Brutal, severe, and showing no pity.

sculpture
The art of carving, especially in stone, or a piece of carved artwork.

soldi
Bronze or silver coins used in Italy.

studio
An artist's workshop.

stylus
A penlike object. The silver stylus stolen by Salaì in the story is a silverpoint—a drawing tool made from a fine piece of silver wire attached to a wooden handle. Silverpoints were used on paper with a special white coating.

tapestry
A patterned, handwoven textile used for wall hangings in wealthy people's homes during medieval and Renaissance times.

tempera
A type of paint made by mixing pigment with egg yolk.

tournament
A popular form of entertainment in medieval and Renaissance Europe. Knights would compete on horseback.

Vatican
An area of Rome that includes the pope's royal palace and court buildings.

INDEX

ACKNOWLEDGMENTS

The publisher would like to thank the following for permission to reproduce their material. Every care has been taken to trace copyright holders. However, if there have been unintentional omissions or failure to trace copyright holders, we apologize and will, if informed, endeavor to make corrections in any future edition.

Key: *b* = bottom, *c* = center, *l* = left, *r* = right, *t* = top

Front cover: Bridgeman Art Library (BAL)/Galleria dell'Accademia, Venice; BAL/Private Collection; back cover: Photolibrary/Henry Steadman; 2 Getty/Photonica; 4*tl* Art Archive/Alfredo Dagli Orti; 4*l* iStock; 4*b* DK Images (DK)/York Archaeological Trust for Excavation and Research; 4*tr* Getty/DK; 4 & 5 Getty/Imagebank; 10 Getty/Photonica; 11*tr* iStock; 11*bl* Shutterstock/J. R. Trice; 12*l* Getty/Imagebank; 14*b* Corbis/Bettmann; 15*t* Wellcome Institute of Medicine; 15*bl* DK/Geoff Dann; 15*br* Art Archive/Dagli Orti; 16*t* iStock; 17*bc* Getty/Siri Stafford; 17*br* Getty/Imagebank; 18*tl* Photolibrary; 19 DK/Andy Crawford; 20*tl* (and endpapers) Corbis/Alinari; 22*bl* Bridgeman Art Library (BAL)/Museo Nazionale del Bargello, Florence; 22*bc* Getty/Glowimages; 22*br* Alamy/Corbis; 24*t* Corbis/Alinari; 25*tr* DK/York Archaeological Trust for Excavation and Research; 25*br* Corbis/Alinari; 28 Getty/DK; 30*tl* Getty/Archive Photos; 30*bl* Art Archive/Gianni Dagli Orti; 32*tl* Art Archive/Alfredo Dagli Orti; 32*cl* Art Archive/Alfredo Dagli Orti; 32*bl* Art Archive/Museo Civico, Padua; 34*l* Shutterstock/Dobroslawa Szulc; 36 Getty/DeAgostini; 37*cr* Getty/DK; 37*r* iStock; 38*l* Corbis/Alinari; 38*b* Corbis/Alinari; 49 Antiquarianimages; 50 Corbis/Sergio Pitamitz; 51*tr* Art Archive; 51*br* BAL/Museo Opificio delle Pietre Dure, Florence; 52*bl* BAL/Giraudon; 52*tr* Corbis/The Gallery Collection; 52*br* Art Archive/Musée du Louvre; 53*t* BAL/Charmet; 53*r* BAL/Palazzo Vecchio, Florence; 54*l* Art Archive/British Library; 54*c* Corbis/Jim Sugar; 54*br* Art Archive/Gianni Dagli Orti; 55*tl* Art Archive/Gianni Dagli Orti; 55*tl* Science Photo Library/Mehau Kulyk; 55*tl* Corbis/Bettmann; 55*bl* Scala; 55*tr* Getty/DK; 55*br* Corbis/Bettmann; 56*tl* BAL/Orsanmichele, Florence; 56*bl* Corbis/Art Archive; 56*tr* DK; 56*c* Corbis/Alinari; 57*tr* Corbis/Summerfield Press; 57*b* Corbis/Summerfield Press; 58*tl* Art Archive/Czartorysky Museum, Kraków; 58*tl* Shutterstock/Balaikin; 58*tr* Corbis/Edim Edia; 58*b* DK/Geoff Dann; 59*bl* Art Archive/Alfredo Dagli Orti; 59*bl* Shutterstock/Marc Dietrich; 59*tr* Corbis/Alinari; 60 DK/York Archaeological Trust for Excavation and Research; 62 BAL/Museo Nazionale del Bargello, Florence